Anna Sewell's
The Adventures of Black Beauty

Black Beauty
and
the Runaway Horse

Adapted by I. M. Richardson
Illustrated by Karen Milone

Troll Associates

Library of Congress Cataloging in Publication Data

Richardson, I. M.
    Black Beauty and the runaway horse.

    (Anna Sewell's The adventures of Black Beauty; bk. 2)
    Summary: Black Beauty tells of his experiences at
the Earl's stable, his stint as a ''job horse,'' and his
sale at a horse fair.
    1. Horses—Juvenile fiction. [1. Horses—Fiction]
I. Milone, Karen, ill. II. Sewell, Anna, 1820-1878.
Black Beauty. III. Title. IV. Series: Richardson, I. M.
Anna Sewell's The adventures of Black Beauty; bk. 2
PZ10.3.F413An bk. 2   [Fic]   82-7029
ISBN 0-89375-812-4   AACR2
ISBN 0-89375-813-2 (pbk.)

As soon as I saw my new home, I noticed how grand it was.
There was a fine big house behind a stone gateway, and there
were a number of stables off to the rear. My new master was an
Earl, and a friend of my former owner. His coachman, a man
named York, looked me over carefully when I arrived.

The Earl had bought my friend Ginger and me at the same time, and our stalls were next to one another. The Earl said to York, "When these horses pull the carriage for her ladyship, she will want the bearing reins tight." I had never worn bearing reins, but Ginger said they were horrid. They kept a horse's head up high.

4

The first time my mistress saw us, she was not very pleased. "Tighten those reins," she ordered. York shortened our reins a little more, and I began to feel very uncomfortable. But the worst part was when we came to a hill. I wanted to put my head down and lean into my harness, but I could not. Bearing reins made it hard to pull a carriage, but they were "fashionable."

Day after day, my mistress ordered the reins tightened more and more. Soon they were unbearable. One day, as they were being shortened even more, Ginger reared up so suddenly that York was nearly knocked over. She kept rearing and kicking, and finally, we were unhitched and taken back to the stable. After that, Ginger was no longer used as a carriage horse.

In early spring, my master and mistress went to London, and I was left at home to be used by the rest of the family. Lady Anne liked to go horseback riding, and often rode me. The gentlemen rode either Ginger or a spirited horse named Lizzie. One day, Lady Anne decided that *she* would ride Lizzie. Her cousin, the Colonel, tried to tell her that Lizzie was too nervous a horse. But Lady Anne insisted on riding her.

7

Lizzie and I trotted off toward the village. It was a lovely day for a ride, and our riders seemed to be enjoying themselves. Before long, we reached Doctor Ashley's house, where the Colonel was to deliver a message. The Colonel tied me to the gate, and went inside for a moment. Lady Anne sat in Lizzie's saddle, and hummed a little tune.

8

Across the road there was a meadow, and the gate stood open. A boy was bringing out some horses, and making a great deal of noise. Suddenly, a young colt bolted across the road and bumped into Lizzie's leg. Lizzie gave a sharp kick, and dashed off with Lady Anne still in the saddle. I gave a loud neigh, and began pawing the ground impatiently.

The Colonel came out just in time to see Lizzie disappearing down the road at a gallop. He jumped on my back, and we took chase. The road twisted and turned, and we caught only brief glimpses of Lady Anne and the runaway horse. Then Lizzie left the road, and started out over uneven ground. Suddenly, she came to a wide ditch, and tried to jump across it.

As she landed, Lizzie lost her footing, and Lady Anne was thrown to the ground. I cleared the ditch with one leap, and landed safely on the other side. Lady Anne lay motionless, and the Colonel ran over to her. Meanwhile, two men saw Lizzie running off without a rider, and they managed to catch her. Soon they joined us near Lizzie's fallen rider.

"One of you take the black horse, and tell the doctor to come at once," ordered the Colonel. "Then ride to the Earl's estate, and have them send a carriage for Lady Anne." So one of the men scrambled into my saddle, and I started off at a good pace. He had all he could do just to keep from falling off.

We stopped briefly at Doctor Ashley's, and then galloped all the way home. When the news about Lady Anne became known, everyone started rushing about. A carriage was brought out, and fresh horses were put into harness. Lord George, Anne's brother, raced off on Ginger. One of the grooms took me into the stable and rubbed me down.

It seemed like a long time before Ginger was finally brought back into the stable. After she had been groomed and we were alone, she told me what had happened. "Lord George and I got there just as the doctor rode up," she said. "Lady Anne was put into the carriage and brought home. They said she will be all right."

Two days after Lady Anne's accident, the Colonel came to see me. He patted me and praised me. Then he said to Lord George, "I am sure this horse knew how much danger Annie was in. As we chased after that runaway horse, I could not have held him back if I had wanted to." Then I heard him say that Lady Anne should never think of riding any horse but me.

Soon the Colonel had to go back to the army. Reuben Smith, our head groom, drove him to the station in the carriage. I saw the Colonel put some money into Smith's hand. Then he said, "Take good care of that black horse, and don't let anyone ruin him. Keep him for Lady Anne." Then the Colonel took his bag out of the carriage, and went inside to wait for the train.

16

We took the carriage to the carriage makers, where it was to be completely redone before her ladyship returned from London. Smith took my harness off, and put a saddle on me. Then he rode me to the White Lion Inn. He told the stable boy that I was to be fed, and that he would be back at four o'clock.

At five o'clock, Smith said that he had met some friends, and would not be leaving until six. The stable boy told him that a nail was coming loose in one of my shoes. But Smith replied, "It will be all right until we get home." His voice was unusually rough and loud. He did not return until nine o'clock. Then he climbed into the saddle, and we started home.

Along the way, Smith used his whip to make me gallop down
the darkened road. There were many loose stones, and I could
feel my shoe getting looser. Finally, it came off completely, but
Smith didn't seem to care. Soon my hoof was broken and split.
The pain was so great that I stumbled and fell to my knees.
Smith was thrown headlong onto the road.

I struggled to my feet, and limped to the side of the road. The moon had risen, and I could see Smith lying in the road. He tried to move, and he let out a low groan. After that, he did not move again. When they found us about midnight, Smith was dead. As soon as they saw my hoof and my knees, they knew exactly what had happened.

The horse doctor did all he could for me, but I was not well for a long time. My knees never lost their scars. For two months, I was turned loose in a meadow all by myself. One day another horse joined me. It was Ginger. She had been ruined by hard riding, and needed a long rest. "Look at us," she said. "We are not the horses we used to be."

When the Earl returned from London, he said that he could not keep a horse with knees like mine, so I was sold. I was put on a train that went to a distant city. My new master owned a livery stable, where horses were offered for hire. My stall was not as pleasant as the one I had been used to. But a less-than-perfect stall, I soon learned, was the least of my troubles.

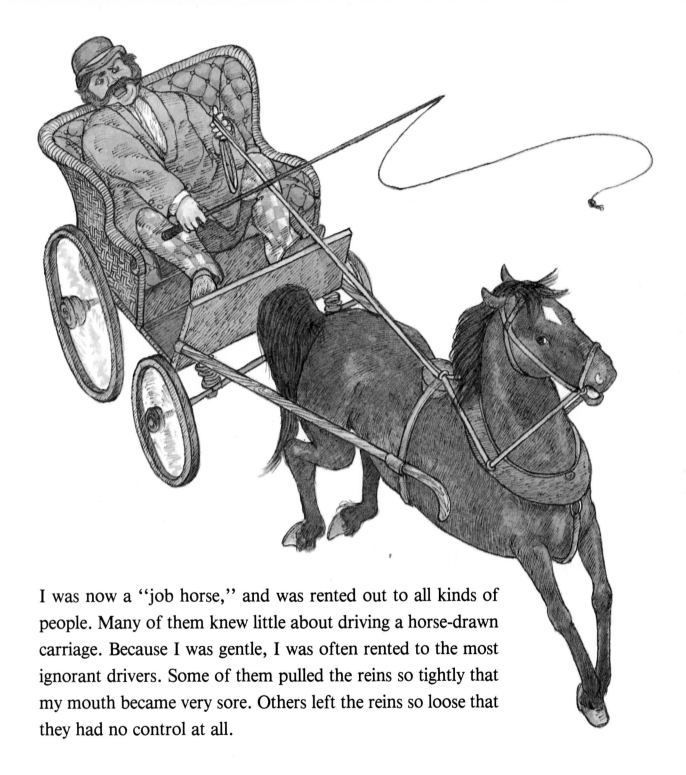

I was now a "job horse," and was rented out to all kinds of people. Many of them knew little about driving a horse-drawn carriage. Because I was gentle, I was often rented to the most ignorant drivers. Some of them pulled the reins so tightly that my mouth became very sore. Others left the reins so loose that they had no control at all.

One day, a family wanted to take a drive in the country. There was a man, a woman, and their two children. As they rode along, they laughed and talked and looked at the scenery. But the man did not drive where the road was smooth, and he did not notice that I had picked up a stone in one of my shoes.

A good driver would have known at once that something was wrong. But this man just laughed, and the stone went deeper and deeper into my hoof. It was very painful. When he finally saw that I was limping, he cried, "Why look! They have rented us a lame horse!" Luckily, a farmer happened by, and he took the time to remove the stone.

Sometimes, I was rented out by the kind of people who are used to traveling by train. They are called "steam-engine drivers," because they think horses are machines. They think we can go as far, move as fast, and pull as heavy a load as they wish. After each day like that, I could hardly make it into my stall for my evening's food and rest.

Once, two gentlemen rented my carriage. I could tell that the one with the reins knew a great deal about horses. So with my neck arched, I set off at my best pace. Later, he tried me several times with the saddle. He liked me, because he talked my owner into selling me to a friend of his. The friend's name was Mr. Barry, and I was to be his first horse.

Mr. Barry ordered the best hay, oats, and corn for me, and he also hired a groom to look after me. I soon realized that I was getting very few of the oats that my master had bought. After two months, I grew very weak. When Mr. Barry's friend saw me again, he said that I should be given more oats, and that the groom should be watched very closely.

Each morning, the groom brought his small son to the stables with him. He put a sack of oats into the boy's covered basket, and sent the boy home. After about a week of this, my master and a police officer came into the stable, and the groom was arrested. He went before the judge and was sent to prison for being a thief.

Mr. Barry's next groom was lazy. He never cleaned my stall, and it began to smell. My feet grew tender from standing on damp straw. One day, as my master rode me into town, my feet hurt so much that I nearly fell down. The blacksmith looked at my hoofs, and ordered my stall to be cleaned out every day. Soon I regained my health and good spirits.

But Mr. Barry was tired of having grooms he could not trust. So I was taken to a horse fair, where I was to be sold. Many people looked at me. But when they saw the scars on my knees, they were not interested. I liked one man who looked at me. He was so gentle that I wished he would buy me. He made an offer, but it was not high enough, and it was refused.

Later, the same man came back again. I reached my head out towards him, and he stroked my face kindly. "Well, old chap," he said. "I think we might get to be good friends." Then he bought me and put a saddle on my back. Half an hour later, we were on our way to London. I knew that with this kind and gentle man for my master, I would be very happy there.